I Want My Potty

Tony Ross

Andersen Press
London

"Nappies are YUUECH!" said the Little Princess. "There MUST be something better!"

This mini edition first published by Andersen Press in 2005.
First published in Great Britain in 1986 by Andersen Press Ltd.,
20 Vauxhall Bridge Road, London SW1V 2SA.
Published in Australia by Random House Australia Pty.,
20 Alfred Street, Milsons Point, Sydney, NSW 2061.
Colour separated in Switzerland by Photolitho AG, Zürich.
Printed and bound in Singapore by Tien Wah Press.

10   9   8   7   6   5   4   3   2   1

British Library Cataloguing in Publication Data available.

ISBN 1 84270 546 6

This paper is made from wood pulp from sustainable forests

"The potty's the place," said the Queen.

At first the Little Princess thought the potty was worse.

"THE POTTY'S THE PLACE!" said the Queen.

So . . . the Little Princess had to learn.

Sometimes the Little Princess was a long way from the potty when she needed it most.

Sometimes the Little Princess played tricks
on the potty . . .

. . . and sometimes the potty played tricks
on the Little Princess.

Soon the potty was fun

and the Little Princess loved it.

Everybody said the Little Princess was clever
and would grow up to be a wonderful queen.

"The potty's the place," said the Little Princess proudly.

One day the Little Princess was playing at the top of the castle . . . when . . .

"I WANT MY POTTY!" she cried.

"She wants her potty," cried the Maid.

"She wants her potty," cried the King.

"She wants her potty," cried the Cook.

"She wants her potty," cried the Gardener.

"She wants her potty," cried the General.

"I know where it is," cried the Admiral.

So the potty was taken as quickly as possible

to the Little Princess . . .

. . . just a little too late.